FABULOUS PERMPY PIG

Illustrated and written by Natasha Curtis

For my partner and our kiddies

This book wouldn't have come together if it wasn't for my partner putting up with my funny five minutes, and supporting me always.

I wouldn't have my child like thoughts if it wasn't for our four amazing kids.

Thankyou to you all for being my life and putting up with me
Love you all more than anything

Permpy pig was so fabulous that her permps didn't bother anyone

She would let them out..
Permps that would just
SHOOT!

Most of them smelt very

BRUTE

Some were so good you could SALUTE

Once it even
killed a tree
down to it's

ROOT

She wished she could normally play the

Instead of music comming out of her

So she tried singing with a microphone,

But all the animals ran and left her alone,

Her voice was screeching and out of tone.

All the animals
were excited to see

PERMPY PIG
PLAYING
HAPPILY

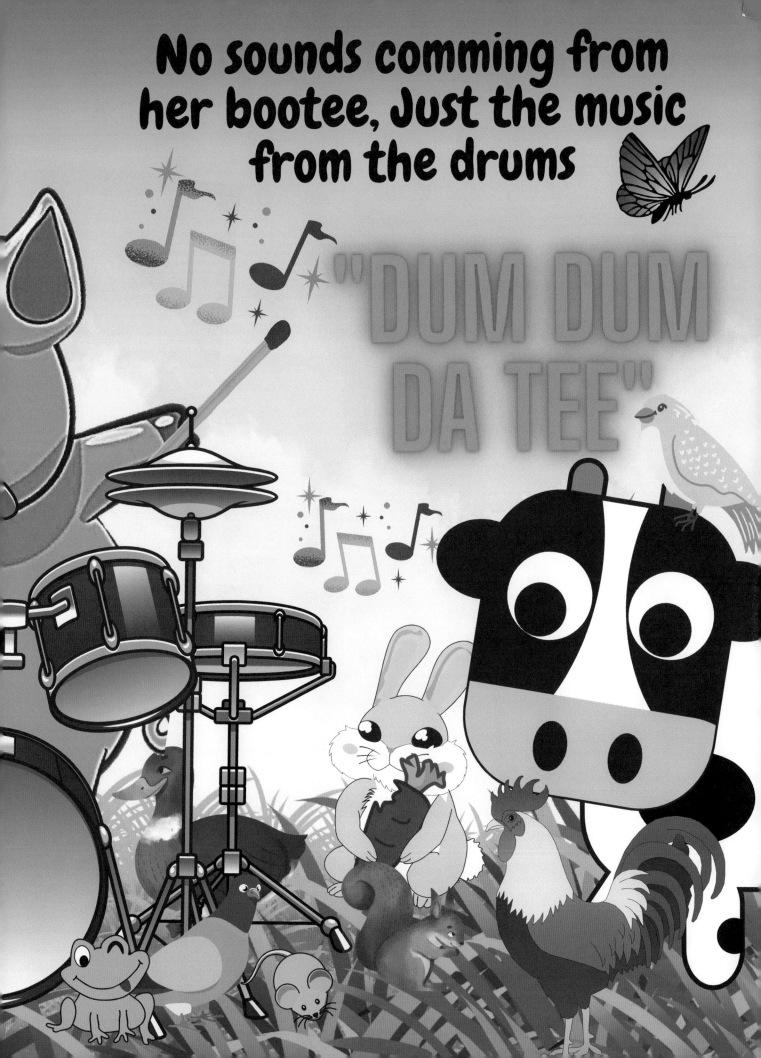

The animals joined in dancing around, Throwing their hands in the air and touching the ground.

COW

FROG

DUCK

MOUSE

PIG

DOG

BUTTERFLY

RABBIT

SWAN

SQUIRREL

A B C D E F G
H I J K L M N
O P Q R S T U
V W X Y Z

1 2 3 4 5
6 7 8 9
10

FABULOUS PERMPY PIG

Illustrated and written
by Natasha Curtis